Dear Parents:

Congratulations! Your child is taking the first steps on an exciting journey. The destination? Independent reading!

STEP INTO READING® will help your child get there. The program offers five steps to reading success. Each step includes fun stories and colorful art or photographs. In addition to original fiction and books with favorite characters, there are Step into Reading Non-Fiction Readers, Phonics Readers and Boxed Sets, Sticker Readers, and Comic Readers—a complete literacy program with something to interest every child.

Learning to Read, Step by Step!

Ready to Read   Preschool–Kindergarten
• big type and easy words • rhyme and rhythm • picture clues
For children who know the alphabet and are eager to begin reading.

Reading with Help   Preschool–Grade 1
• basic vocabulary • short sentences • simple stories
For children who recognize familiar words and sound out new words with help.

Reading on Your Own   Grades 1–3
• engaging characters • easy-to-follow plots • popular topics
For children who are ready to read on their own.

Reading Paragraphs   Grades 2–3
• challenging vocabulary • short paragraphs • exciting stories
For newly independent readers who read simple sentences with confidence.

Ready for Chapters   Grades 2–4
• chapters • longer paragraphs • full-color art
For children who want to take the plunge into chapter books but still like colorful pictures.

STEP INTO READING® is designed to give every child a successful reading experience. The grade levels are only guides; children will progress through the steps at their own speed, developing confidence in their reading.

Remember, a lifetime love of reading starts with a single step!

Published in the United States by Random House Children's Books, a division of Penguin Random House LLC, 1745 Broadway, New York, NY 10019, and in Canada by Penguin Random House Canada Limited, Toronto.

Step into Reading, Random House, and the Random House colophon are registered trademarks of Penguin Random House LLC.

Visit us on the Web!
rhcbooks.com

Educators and librarians, for a variety of teaching tools, visit us at RHTeachersLibrarians.com

ISBN 978-0-593-70972-6 (trade) — ISBN 978-0-593-70973-3 (lib. bdg.)

Printed in the United States of America
10 9 8 7 6 5 4 3 2 1

Barbie

YOU CAN BE A BALLERINA

adapted by Kristen L. Depken
based on the story by Victoria Saxon
illustrated by Mattel

Random House 🏠 New York

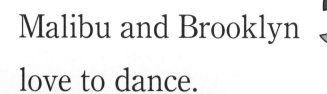

Malibu and Brooklyn
love to dance.
They are ready
for ballet class.
They want to be
ballerinas one day.

The friends line up
for class.
Their teacher is
Ms. Rita.

She shows them
ballet poses.
The girls follow her.

Malibu leaps.

Brooklyn stands
on her toes.

Brooklyn tries
a turn.
It is hard.
She does well!

Malibu practices
the same turn.
She almost falls!

Ms. Rita tells Malibu
to keep trying.

Brooklyn says
she will help.

All week,
Brooklyn and Malibu
practice together.
Brooklyn helps Malibu.

They try the turn
in class.
They both do
a great job!

Ms. Rita asks the girls
if they would like to visit
the city ballet company.
They say yes.

The next day, the girls go
to the city ballet company.

They meet Linda.

She is a ballerina.

19

Linda brings them
to meet more dancers.
They invite the girls
to practice.

Linda shows the girls
the dressing room.
There are so many
pretty costumes!

It is time
for practice.
Brooklyn and Malibu
join the other dancers.

Everyone is
warming up.

Ms. Isabelle arrives.
She is the city
ballet teacher.

She helps the dancers
with their steps.

The dancers move
their arms.
They bend their legs
and point their toes.

Next,
the dancers leap.
Malibu tries it.
She does great!

27

The dancers practice
for a show.
Linda asks the girls
to be in the show, too!

Malibu and
Brooklyn say yes.
They practice
on the stage.

Brooklyn gets
a purple costume.
Malibu gets
a pink one.

It is showtime!

The girls dancc

in the ballet.

They are so happy!

31

"You can be a ballerina!"

  says Malibu.

"So can you!"

  says Brooklyn.

Dear Parents:

Congratulations! Your child is taking the first steps on an exciting journey. The destination? Independent reading!

STEP INTO READING® will help your child get there. The program offers five steps to reading success. Each step includes fun stories and colorful art or photographs. In addition to original fiction and books with favorite characters, there are Step into Reading Non-Fiction Readers, Phonics Readers and Boxed Sets, Sticker Readers, and Comic Readers—a complete literacy program with something to interest every child.

Learning to Read, Step by Step!

Ready to Read Preschool–Kindergarten
• big type and easy words • rhyme and rhythm • picture clues
For children who know the alphabet and are eager to begin reading.

Reading with Help Preschool–Grade 1
• basic vocabulary • short sentences • simple stories
For children who recognize familiar words and sound out new words with help.

Reading on Your Own Grades 1–3
• engaging characters • easy-to-follow plots • popular topics
For children who are ready to read on their own.

Reading Paragraphs Grades 2–3
• challenging vocabulary • short paragraphs • exciting stories
For newly independent readers who read simple sentences with confidence.

Ready for Chapters Grades 2–4
• chapters • longer paragraphs • full-color art
For children who want to take the plunge into chapter books but still like colorful pictures.

STEP INTO READING® is designed to give every child a successful reading experience. The grade levels are only guides; children will progress through the steps at their own speed, developing confidence in their reading.

Remember, a lifetime love of reading starts with a single step!

Published in the United States by Random House Children's Books, a division of Penguin Random House LLC, 1745 Broadway, New York, NY 10019, and in Canada by Penguin Random House Canada Limited, Toronto.

Step into Reading, Random House, and the Random House colophon are registered trademarks of Penguin Random House LLC.

Visit us on the Web!
StepIntoReading.com
rhcbooks.com

Educators and librarians, for a variety of teaching tools, visit us at RHTeachersLibrarians.com

ISBN 978-0-593-70972-6 (trade) — ISBN 978-0-593-70973-3 (lib. bdg.)

Printed in the United States of America
10 9 8 7 6 5 4 3 2 1

YOU CAN BE A GYMNAST

adapted by Kristen L. Depken
based on a story by Gabrielle Reyes
illustrated by Susanna Amati and Mattel

Random House 🏠 New York

Malibu and Brooklyn
love gymnastics.
They want to be gymnasts.

They go to class
with their friends.
There is a big
meet next week.

Coach Maria
helps them
get ready.

Malibu swings.

Brooklyn flips.

Daisy does
a backflip.

Brooklyn tries
a handstand.

Coach Maria

gives them tips.

Malibu and Brooklyn
are excited for the meet.

Brooklyn practices
on the bars.
Malibu helps.

The girls work together.
Coach Maria
is proud.

Malibu practices her moves.

She leaps.

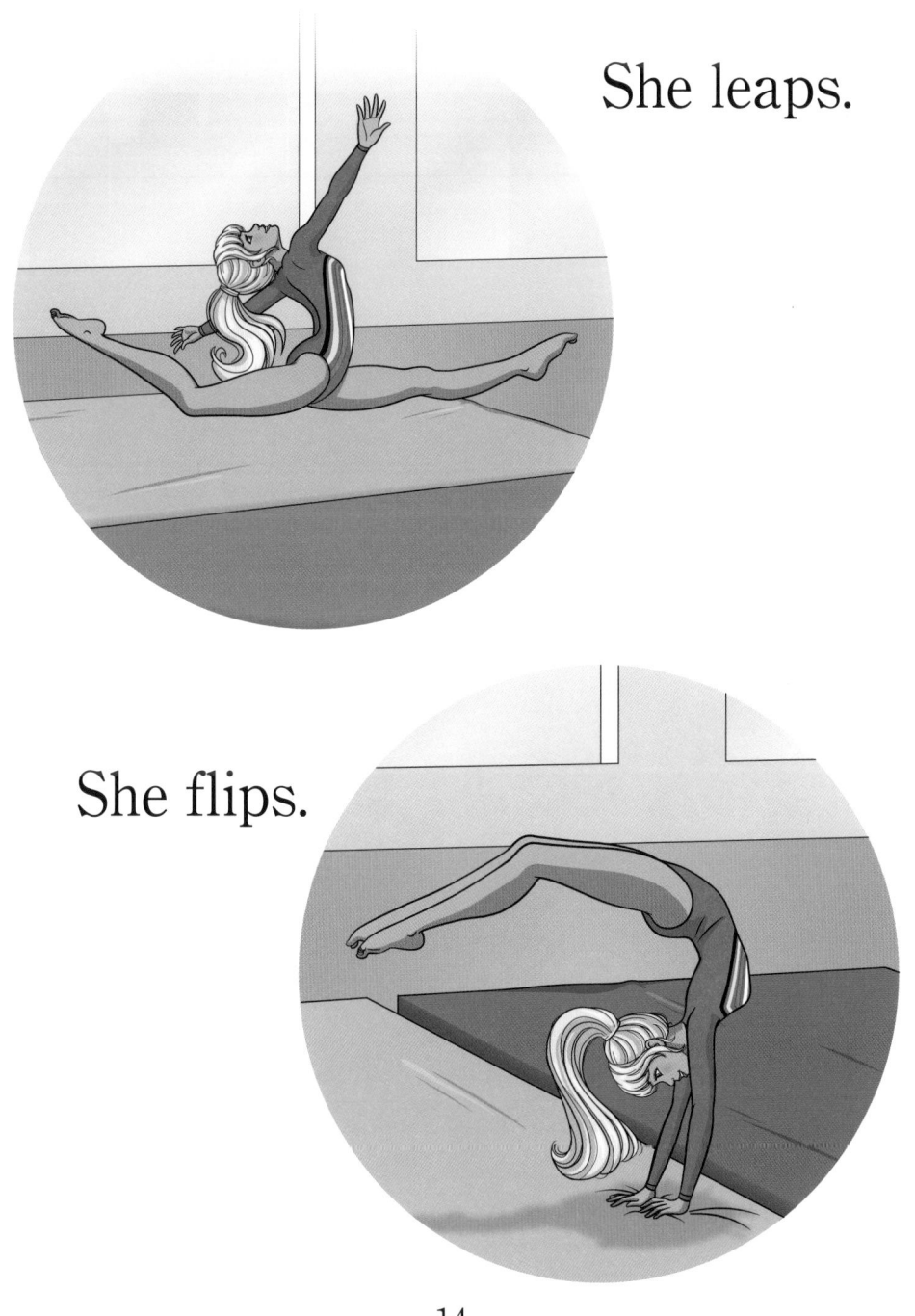

She flips.

Malibu falls
on the mat.
"You can do it,"
says Coach Maria.

Brooklyn tries a flip
on the bar.

She stumbles
when she lands.

"Keep trying,"
says Coach Maria.
"You're doing great!"

Malibu and Brooklyn
work together
every day.

It is time
for the meet!
The team is ready.

Malibu goes first.

Malibu stands.

She leaps.

She twists.

She does a backflip.

Her routine is perfect!

The team cheers.

Nikki is next.
She springs
in the air.
Malibu cheers.

Daisy is on the beam.

She does a handstand.

"Great job!"

says Brooklyn.

Brooklyn goes next.
She swings
on the bars.

She lands.

It is perfect!

The judges give everyone
a score.

The girls' team wins!

Brooklyn and

Malibu hug.

Coach Maria is proud.

The friends jump for joy.

They cheer.

They give high fives.

"You make
    a great team!"
    says Coach Maria.

"You can be a gymnast!"
says Malibu.
"So can you!"
says Brooklyn.